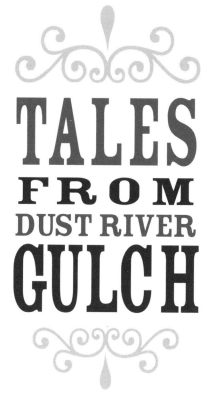

TALES FROM DUST RIVER GULCH

TIM DAVIS

JOURNEYFORTH

Greenville, South Carolina

Library of Congress Cataloging-in-Publication Data

Davis, Tim, 1957–
    Tales from Dust River Gulch / Tim Davis.
        p. cm.
    Contents: Showdown — Billy the Kid — Gold in that thar soup —
Doc Hardly — Hare-rasin' horseshoes — End of the rodeo.
    ISBN 0-89084-896-3
    [1. Sheriffs—Fiction.   2. Robbers and outlaws—Fiction.
3. Frontier and pioneer life—West (U.S.)—Fiction.   4. West (U.S.)—
Fiction.]   I. Title.
PZ7.D3179Tal   1997   96-38576
[Fic]—dc20   CIP
                                                                        AC

Tales from Dust River Gulch

Project Editor: Debbie L. Parker

Cover and illustrations by Tim Davis

© 1996 by BJU Press
Greenville, SC 29614
JourneyForth Books is a division of BJU

ISBN 978-0-89084-896-8

15   14   13   12   11   10   9   8   7   6   5   4

To Joshua Davis—
my own little J.D.

Books illustrated by Tim Davis

Pocket Change
Grandpa's Gizmos
The Cranky Blue Crab
Once in Blueberry Dell

Books written and illustrated by Tim Davis

Mice of the Herring Bone
Mice of the Nine Lives
Mice of the Seven Seas
Tales from Dust River Gulch

CONTENTS

WANTED

GRUFFLE O'BUFFALO

GUILTY OF CRIMES AGAINST THE PEOPLE:

Cattle Rustling, Swindling, Illegal Branding,
Thieving, Lying, Cheating, Loitering,
Humiliating Law Enforcement Agents,
Etc., Etc.

CHAPTER 1
Showdown

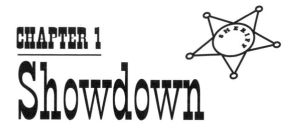

Now don't git the notion that the folks in Dust River Gulch were a bunch of softies. Nothin' could be further from the truth. Dust River Gulch was inhabited by some of the wildest characters west of the Mississippi. Few human-type outlaws would test a town whose sheriff was a thoroughbred mustang. But this here Gruffle O'Buffalo—now there was a different sort of outlaw. He was wanted in seventy-eight counties an' half a dozen zoos. It was no wonder the folks of Dust River Gulch were feelin' a mite queasy when they heard he'd be passin' through.

It wasn't that folks didn't have confidence in Sheriff J.D. Saddlesoap. No doubt about it, he was an awe-inspirin' figure—a mighty good lawman an' a fine-lookin' horse to boot. Many's the wild an' woolly outlaws he'd driven out of town. But, ya see, this was different. This was Gruffle O'Buffalo.

Well, seems as if it was old Tumbleweeze McPhearson that mostly started stirrin' up the townsfolk. Over at Rosie's Restaurant, he was a-gobblin' down some grub when he leaked out the rumor.

"Yep, 'bout this time tomorrow, I reckon most folks'll be sittin' in their houses with the doors bolted up."

Old Bo, the lizard, leaned over from the next table. "Whatcha talkin' 'bout, Weeze?"

"Nothin' other than Gruffle O'Buffalo an' his gang of bum steers," replied old Tumbleweeze with a snort.

"Gruffle O'Buffalo!" Old Bo got so startled that he dropped his spoon–*perclunk.*

Well, the murmurin' started up mighty quick-like all through the restaurant. 'Fore long every ear in the house was tuned in to old Tumbleweeze. (It was the usual way news got around in Dust River Gulch.)

The old weasel continued, "Yep, word has it old Gruff an' his gang are comin' to town tomorrow."

"Tomorrow?" squealed Rosie, who kept the restaurant as tidy as her own kitchen. "Somebody go git J.D.!"

While a wild-eyed prairie dog went a-scamperin' after Sheriff Saddlesoap, Old Tumbleweeze kept on a-stirrin' up the folk.

"I heard the last town old Gruff an' his gang passed through, the folks haven't nearly recovered yet."

While some folks were tremblin' an' whisperin', Bo asked, "Why haven't they?"

"Well, he an' his gang done humiliated the sheriff an' his deputies so bad that they hightailed it outta town. So then the folks were so scared they just did whatever old Gruff asked 'em." Tumbleweeze paused to munch a spell. "Nearly stole the town blind, they did."

A scrawny buzzard asked, "You think Sheriff J.D. can take 'em on?"

Tumbleweeze shrugged. "I don't know. Gruff's ruined plenty of sheriffs in his day."

Well, at that comment, the mutterin' an' murmurin' got near a deafenin' pitch there at Rosie's Restaurant. Some folks were sayin' they'd been a-plannin' to be out of town the next day anyway. An' the rest started makin' such-like plans.

But Miss Rosie, she wouldn't have none of it. She started a-scoldin' an' a-shamin' those folks fer not trustin' in Sheriff J.D. like they should've. 'Course, everybody knew she had a sweet spot in her heart fer J.D., but they took the scoldin' to heart anyways.

The little lady kept on a-going. "Why, he's the finest, bravest sheriff you'll find in any county, anyplace! No outlaw's gonna run him outta this town! No, not J.D."

Then the doors swung open. In walked none other than Sheriff J.D. Saddlesoap himself. "Why, thank ya, Miss Rosie. That's mighty sweet of ya."

Miss Rosie turned sorta pink-like as J.D. smiled over at her. "Well, it's true, isn't it, J.D.?" she said. "You're gonna stand up to that there Gruffle O'Buffalo an' his gang, aren't you?"

J.D.'s smile looked a mite strained, an' he swallowed mighty hard. But he said he would. If nothin' else, he wouldn't make Miss Rosie into a liar.

Well, tomorrow came a mite sooner than Sheriff J.D. was a-hopin'. Seemed like most folks decided to stay in town after all, seein' as how Sheriff J.D. was a-gonna stand up to Gruff an' his gang. They weren't about to miss that, now were they?

Round about noontime, old Tumbleweeze was out in the street with his ear to the ground. Lots of folks was a-watchin' real quiet-like. Perty soon he spoke up. "They's a-comin'! I kin hear the rumble!"

Everybody cleared the street an' waited. They was a-lookin' out winders an' peerin' 'round barrels. Rosie's Restaurant was jammed with folks, eatin' an' strainin' their necks to see 'round each other outside.

No doubt about it, that cloud of dust on the horizon was gittin' closer every second.

J.D. was a-waitin'. He wouldn't start no trouble—but as sure as he'd promised Miss Rosie, he wouldn't stand fer none either.

So into Dust River Gulch they came—old Gruffle O'Buffalo an' his gang of bum steers. They did a little hootin' an' hollerin', an' then they headed to Rosie's.

Everybody was actin' as calm as they could inside—but most folk were sweatin' like it was two hundred degrees. Then in sauntered Gruff an' his steers.

"We's hot!" rumbled the big, mangy buffalo. He turned to Rosie, standing behind the stove. "You there, give m' boys some milk shakes."

Rosie went right to it an' served those five bum steers real quick-like. They started a-slurpin' an' a-sloppin' it like the no 'count critters they were. Meanwhile, ol' Gruff, he was a-saunterin' 'round the place like he was king. He plucked the cherry right off the top of one buzzard's sundae. Gruff smiled an' rubbed his straggly-lookin' beard whiles he ate that cherry.

The buzzard didn't say nothin'. Fact is, the only sound in the place was the slurpin' an' sloppin' of those bum steers, startin' in on their second round of milk shakes.

Finally, Gruff seemed 'bout strutted out, an' he found a table to his likin'. So old Gruff, he took a seat. Poor old Bo, the lizard, he was already a-sittin' at that same table. Gruff sorta gave him the eye an' rumbled, "I prefers a private table, myself." An' Bo, he pert near melted to the floor an' slithered over to the next table whiles Gruff chuckled to himself.

"Hey, gal," Gruff yelled out real sudden-like. "I's ready to order." So Rosie, she hustled on over to his table. "Give me a gallon of the sourest, smelliest, most curdled-up milk ya got," growled the shaggy outlaw.

There was some quiet-like oohin' and ahhin' at that, an' Gruff sat back in his chair with a satisfied snort.

Then Rosie said, "Only *one* gallon, sir?" in a smart-alecky sorta way.

Gruff, he raised himself up and rumbled out, "Nah, make it *three* gallons, gal! An' quick-like!"

Perty soon Rosie came back with the sourest milk you ever smelt! Gruffle sorta chuckled an' drank it all down like it was nothin' to him. Course, everybody at Rosie's couldn't hardly believe it.

The old buffalo let out with a hiccup an' yelled over to his gang of bum steers (still a-slurpin' an' a-sloppin'), "C'mon, boys! We's a-goin'!"

So the whole bunch of 'em started fer the door. Most of the folks started breathin' normal-like again—that is, till Miss Rosie spoke up. She said, "Sir, you an' your boys haven't paid your bill."

Then Old Gruff turned around real slow-like an' looked Rosie in the eye. An' it got quiet—terrible quiet. Then the bum steers started a-laughin' an' a-snortin' like nobody's business, an' out the door they went. And Gruffle, he started a-saunterin' out too.

Then Rosie (she was a mighty plucky lady) said flat out, "Sir, you haven't paid."

The bum steers couldn't hardly take it, they were laughin' so hard. Old Gruff strutted over to poor old Bo an' picked him up by the kerchief an' set him on a table by Rosie. He blew out some sour milk breath and said, "My friend here says he'll pay." An' the bum steers started a-howlin' with laughter.

But the laughin' didn't last long this time. 'Cause who do you think came through the swingin' doors? None other than Sheriff J.D. Saddlesoap.

Gruffle smiled an' said, "Well, if it ain't the sheriff!"

J.D. just looked at Rosie an' asked, "What's the trouble here, Miss Rosie?"

Rosie told him, whiles Gruffle sorta snickered an' rubbed his mangy beard. The bum steers, gittin' mighty interested in the goings-on, sauntered back into Rosie's. One of the mangiest of 'em spoke up. "Whatcha gonna do about it, Sheriff?"

J.D. puffed up his chest an' replied, "Gruffle, you're not gittin' away with anything in Dust River Gulch. Pay up an' git outta town."

Gruff sauntered over till he was 'most in J.D.'s face an' breathed out sour milk breath. "Who's gonna make me, Sheriff?"

"You're lookin' at him."

Well, Gruff, he started smilin' an' rubbin' that mangy beard of his.

"Maybe we can make a deal with this here sheriff, eh, boys?"

The bums a-snorted an' a-snickered. "Yeah, boss. Maybe."

"You boys want a little entertainment?"

"Yeah, boss!"

Gruffle smiled real mean-like an' said, "How 'bout we have ourselves a little rodeo, Sheriff, just you an' me?"

"What're you sayin', Gruff?" asked the sheriff, and the steers commenced their laughin' again.

"We'll have a rodeo. You ride me an' I ride you. An' the one who stays on the longest is the winner, see?"

Well, now, that mangy buffalo musta had nearly a thousand pounds on J.D., but one glance in Miss Rosie's direction, an' the sheriff figured he'd accept the challenge. "If I win, you'll pay up an' git outta town, right?"

Gruffle snorted his approval. "Gladly, Sheriff. But now, if you might just happen to lose, you'll do the same?"

J.D. nodded.

"That is, if you kin still walk." At that, the bum steers started a-snickerin' an' a-snortin' like nobody's business again.

"Let's go, Sheriff," grunted Gruff.

So out went the outlaw an' the lawman, followed real close-like by the snickerin' steers. An' then 'most the whole town gathered 'round in front of Rosie's Restaurant.

Gruffle and J.D., they stood on opposite sides of the street, a-loosenin' up an' eyein' each other real fearsome-like. They decided old Tumbleweeze would keep time, along with one of the smarter bum steers (or at least one of the less dumb ones, that is). J.D. would ride Gruffle first, then vicey-versey.

Gruffle, he had a sneaky, sly sorta smile on his face like he was up to somethin'. An' wouldn't you know it—he was. When nobody was a-payin' no mind, he slipped one of the spurs off his boot an' hid it in the thick, mangy hair on his back, real secret-like. He whispered what he'd done to his no 'count steers, and they started some fearsome snickerin'.

Meanwhile, J.D. was developin' a perty sizable lump in his throat. He hadn't never ridden no buffalo before. Specially not when it counted fer so much.

Miss Rosie, she musta sensed it, 'cause she ran over to him an' planted a big, sweet kiss on the end of his nose an' said, sweet as anything, "Whup him, J.D.!"

With a spark in his eye, Sheriff J.D. Saddlesoap called out, "I'm ready, Gruffle! Are you?"

Gruffle O'Buffalo, he smiled an' snorted out, "Yep." An' there he stood, ready to be ridden.

All the folks held their breath. Then J.D. galloped over an' hopped onta Gruffle's back.

"Start a-timin', Weeze," called Miss Rosie. An' he did.

The mangy outlaw started a-buckin' an' a-snortin'. He ran 'round in a circle front-wise an' back, sendin' some folks fer cover. Up he reared an' down he tramped, whiles J.D. was bouncin' 'round on his back like a jackrabbit.

"Ride'm, J.D.!"

"Yahoo!"

"Whup'm, Sheriff!"

"Ride him right outta town!"

Meanwhiles, the bum steers was a-snickerin' a mite less. But Gruff was a-snortin' up a storm. He was a-twistin' in contortions an' a-kickin' like a mad billy goat.

J.D. was a-feeling like a sack of pataters that's been bounced downstairs, but he was still a-holdin' on. Then he hit that spur.

"Yee-ooowww!"

The spur sent J.D. up past the roof of Rosie's, an' down he landed in a cloud of dust. But one glance in the direction of his favorite gal, an' he claimed he was just feelin' a mite sore.

"One minute an' forty-two seconds!" announced Tumbleweeze.

Old Bo, the lizard, was so excited, that he yelled, "Beat that, you outlaw, you!"

But Gruffle, he shuffled over to Bo's face an' blew out enough sour milk breath to send old Bo into a coughin' fit.

"Heh, heh." Gruffle turned to J.D. an' snorted. "Yer next, Sheriff. Now I ride you."

So J.D., he dusted himself off and stood in position, still a-catchin' his breath.

Gruffle reared up an' took a flyin' leap onto J.D.'s back. Whomp! J.D. was squished as flat on his face as a bearskin rug.

"Start a-timin', weasel," chuckled Gruffle. An' he did.

Thirty seconds went by, an' the bum steers was all smiles. Ya see, Sheriff Saddlesoap hadn't got up off his face yet.

"C'mon, J.D.!"

"Buck him, Sheriff! Buck him!"

"Git up, J.D. You can git him yet!"

The bum steers was a-laughin' like nobody's business by now 'cause J.D. was still a-squirmin' underneath the big buffalo.

But how was old Gruff a-doin'? Seemed like he shoulda been laughin' louder than them all. But he weren't. Nope, instead he was a-lookin' kinda greenish.

One of the bum steers noticed it. "What's wrong with the boss?"

"Dunno. He's lookin' mighty queasy, though."

An' sure 'nuff, he was. His face was a-puckerin' an' a-twitchin'. Seems like that three gallons of sour milk had got mighty churned up. He was groanin' an' moanin' an' holdin'

his stomach. Then he let out with a hiccup and rolled right off J.D.'s back, howlin' like a shot coyote.

Folks' mouths dropped open. They was so shook up they couldn't hardly say nothin'.

Sudden-like, over the moanin' of the sickly buffalo, old Tumbleweeze spoke up an' said, "One minute an' twenty-nine seconds."

Then what a ruckus there was! All kinds of cheerin' an' yellin'!

"You did it, J.D.!"

"You won!"

"Way to whup him, Sheriff!"

J.D., he stood himself up an' brushed off the dust. Folks was jumpin' 'round him an' shakin' his hoof, congratulatin' him like he was a livin' legend or somethin'.

Seein' as how they was licked fair an' square, the bum steers started sorta sneakin' outta town with their moanin' boss slung over their shoulders.

"Hey, boys," yelled out Rosie. "You haven't paid!"

"Ain't paid!" shouted some old prairie dog. "Why, we oughta tar an' feather 'em!"

"That's too good fer 'em," yelled Bo. "We'll let J.D. take 'em on!"

"Yeah, but let me git a piece of 'em first," hollered some burly mountain goat.

The bum steers emptied out their pockets as quick as a flash an' started runnin' like fresh-branded cattle clear outta Dust River Gulch.

An' the cheerin' and the celebratin' commenced all over again. The folks carried J.D. into the restaurant. 'Most everybody wanted to buy him a sundae or a shake or some such-like thing.

"Don't spoil his appetite now," said Rosie, "'cause I'm gonna cook him the best-tastin' supper he ever laid eyes on."

She glanced kinda shy-like over at J.D. "That is, if'n he'll accept my invitation to supper."

"Miss Rosie," replied the Sheriff, "I wouldn't miss it fer nothin'."

Well, nowadays, whiles they're a-slurpin' down their milk shakes at Rosie's Restaurant, folks still listen to old Tumbleweeze tell 'bout the time old Gruffle O'Buffalo an' his gang of bum steers came to town. An' Rosie, she keeps plenty of sour milk on hand, just in case.

WANTED

BILLY THE KID

GUILTY OF CRIMES AGAINST THE PEOPLE:

Vandalism, Smashing, Tromping, Eating Clothes,
Butting into Innocent Bystanders, General Orneriness,
Humiliating Law Enforcement Agents,
Etc., Etc.

CHAPTER 2
Billy the Kid

Now Dust River Gulch always has been a dandy place to live, fer law-abidin' folks, that is. An' there ain't no sheriff west of the Mississippi with a better pedigree than the Gulch's own J.D. Saddlesoap. He's a fine-lookin' mustang, an' his heart's tender as a bare foot in a cactus patch.

But he don't tolerate no trouble in town. No siree. No tellin' how many outlaws he's run out. Let's see now, there were Trigger McGee an' Cactus-Face Curt, Snake-eye Smith an' the Buzzard-Breath Kid. An' who could forget what he done to Gruffle O'Buffalo an' his gang of bum steers? That rodeo showdown nearly made J.D. Saddlesoap into a livin' legend! But of course, you done heard that story by now.

Well, one particular morning, ol' Tumbleweeze McPhearson was slurpin' down his first cup of coffee at Rosie's Restaurant. "Goooood coffee, Rosie," he said.

Rosie answered kinda shy-like, "Why, thankee, Tumble—"

When what do ya think? There came a billy goat, kickin' out the front winder of the restaurant! *Ker-SMASH!* Jest like that!

"Yee-oww!" Tumbleweeze shot up outta his seat like he were settin' on a brandin' iron. His coffee showered everbody in the place.

"Why the nerve of that goat!" said Rosie. "I'm goin' fer the sheriff!" An' she stormed over to J.D.'s office.

By the time Rosie got in, there was 'bout a dozen other townsfolk in there a-complainin' already. J.D.'s c was noisy as a cattle barn 'fore milkin' time.

"That goat done ate my best bloomers right off'n th clothesline!" sobbed Mrs. Holstein.

"An' he tramped all over my fresh-mended roof," added Bo, the lizard. "He kin climb up most anythin'!"

"My best britches been chewed through," said Cyrus the Skunk. He scowled at his wife and said, "Don't see why ya warshed 'em anyways." Then the two of 'em commenced arguin'.

"Hold everthing, folks!" J.D. said. "Who's the culprit doin' all this?"

"That goat!" yelled everbody at once.

"Said his name was Billy," explained Bo. "Billy the Kid."

Well J.D.'s eyes got mighty big, an' he swallered kinda hard. Now you mighta heard tell 'bout a feller by the name of Billy the Kid yerself. 'Course it probably weren't the same feller. Ya see, this Billy was a real hoof-stompin', horn-headed, cud-chewin' kid—I mean a real mountain goat!

So ya cain't blame J.D. fer feelin' a mite taken back.

Then the complainin' commenced again. Curly the arma-dillo was rubbin' his head.

"That Billy feller," said Curly, "he came chargin' down the street an' butted me in the head, Sheriff. An' that set me rollin' like a bowlin' ball—SMASH—inta the cracker-barrel by the general store."

Then J.D. laid eyes on Rosie in the back of the room. An' there was a teardrop rollin' down that perty cheek of hers. "What's that billy goat done to you, Rosie?" he asked, real tender-like.

Rosie sniffed a little an' said, "He kicked out my front winder—smashed it to smithereens!"

Now nobody messes with Rosie, not if J.D. Saddlesoap has anythin' to say about it. He slammed his hoof down on his desk. "I'm mad enough to sting a hornet," he said. "I'm goin' after that outlaw right now!" An' he did, quick as a jackrabbit.

Well, that good-fer-nothin' goat, he had climbed his way up to the roof of Rosie's place. "Har, har, Sheriff!" he hooted an' hollered. "Jest see if'n you kin git me up here!"

Now there ain't nothin' worse than a gloatin' goat. So J. D. took a deep breath an' said, "You cain't git away from me that easy, you lowdown excuse fer a mountain goat." Then he climbed his way up after him.

Billy, he jumped on over to the next roof an' commenced his hootin' an' hollerin again. J.D. took a runnin' start, an' he did the same. So that mountain goat took a leap over to the next rooftop. An' J.D., he tried to foller. But he came up a bit short, an' he ended up hangin' onta the edge of a windersill instead. Well, the sheriff didn't give up easy—he kicked an' pulled himself up inta the winder an' found the stairs up to the roof. So the chase was on again!

Well, this went on fer some time, with the two of 'em jumpin' an' chasin' from roof to roof. Perty soon the whole town was watchin' an' cheerin' on the sheriff.

"C'mon J.D.—Get him!" they said.

"Oh, J.D., please be careful!" (That was Rosie.)

An' they were a-hootin' an' a-whistlin' the whole time.

Then Billy, he climbed right up the flagpole of the Dust River Gulch Post Office an' perched himself on top. J.D. wasn't discouraged; he jest shimmied his way up the pole, inch by inch, closin' the gap.

The town folks cheered. "Ya got him cornered, Sheriff!"

But jest as J.D. got close enough to take a swipe at Billy, that goat reared back his head an' butted him right under the chin.

The sheriff fell back, all the way down, an' right into a waterin' trough—*kersplash!*

The town folks looked mighty discouraged. An' old Tumbleweeze added insult to injury when he said, "Sheriff, ya ain't never let us down before." Folks were murmerin' an' mumblin' an' shakin' their heads.

Rosie stayed behind to help J.D. outta that thar waterin' trough. "You'll git him yet, J.D.," she said.

An' Billy? He jest laughed himself silly. "Hey, Sheriff, are ya thirsty?" he yelled. An' he laughed so hard he pert near fell off the flagpole.

Now J.D. knew he had to come up with a better plan. "A little breakfast might give me some food fer thought, Rosie," he said. So he sloshed his way back to Rosie's Restaurant an' set himself down at the counter.

A couple of other fellers kinda moved down a ways. "Old J.D. ain't got what it takes to catch a billy goat, huh?" they snorted.

See, the folks 'round here ain't used to havin' their sheriff eat humble pie. Like Tumbleweeze said—J.D., he ain't never let 'em down before.

"Ba-a-a-hh!" said some old skunk, pretending to butt at J.D. from across the room.

"Don't pay them no mind," Rosie said. "I'll fix ya a nice mess of grits an' you'll be up an' at it again."

Well J.D., he was grateful fer the grits a-cookin', an' specially fer Rosie's faith in him. Perty soon, Rosie scooped up a mustang-size helpin' of grits outta her big black skillet an' set 'em down at J.D.'s place, steamin' hot.

"Thank ya, Rosie," he said. "I'm much obliged."

Whiles J.D. was eatin', he heard that goat trampin' on the roof again. "He's about as hard to catch as greased pig on a rainy day," sighed the tuckered horse.

"Hmmm," said Rosie, scratchin' her perty head. "Maybe ya ain't got to catch him."

"Why he'll ruin the town if I don't," snorted J.D.

"What I mean is, ya got to let him catch himself."

"How's that?"

"Well, what's that goat like to do best?"

"I 'magine it's humiliatin' me," sighed J.D.

"Maybe so," said Rosie, an' she commenced a-scrubbin' out her big black skillet. Then she brought that skillet over an' shoved it to J.D. on the sly. "Try puttin' this in yer hat," she said.

"This?" said J.D. "Why it's tough enough to be a war helmet!"

"Jest try it," said Rosie with a wink. "An' keep yer head low."

A few minutes later, here came J.D., trudgin' outta the restaurant. His head was a-hangin'. Some of the town folks were sneerin'. It looked like the sheriff done give up all together.

Well, 'round the corner, Billy the Kid peered out. He wasn't about to miss a chance to kick a feller when he's down. So he came a-chargin'. He had his head lowered an' was comin' full steam, aimin' right fer the sheriff's hung-down head.

"Look out, sheriff!" yelled old Bo, but the sheriff didn't even look up. Billy was comin' like a runaway train—closer an' closer.

He hit J.D. smack in the hat—CLANK!

It sounded like that goat done rung the bell in town square. It was such a peculiar sound, that clank. An' Billy, he bounced back like a rubber ball an' went limp. Would you believe it? That mountain goat collapsed in the middle of the street!

"Well, ain't that somethin'?" Bo gasped. Meanwhiles everbody else was plum speechless.

J.D. dusted himself off an' jest slung Billy over his shoulder like a knapsack.

"It's back to the mountains fer you, Billy," he said.

From her broken winder, Rosie, she jest looked out a-smilin' as the sheriff toted that goat away. An' folks 'round here, they still claim Sheriff J.D.'s as hardheaded as they come.

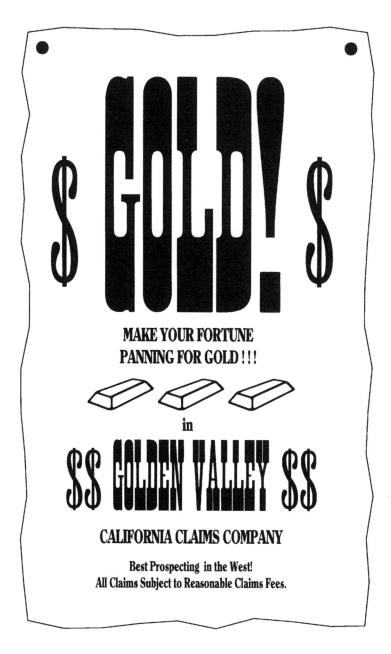

CHAPTER 3

Gold in That Thar Soup

Now Dust River Gulch never had been much of a place fer keepin' secrets. Most everbody knew that. News got 'round perty quick-like, specially at Rosie's Restaurant. Tryin' to keep a secret in there at lunchtime was, well, like tryin' to hide a skunk-skin in yer back pocket on a hot day. Folks tended to sniff it out. Old Bo, the lizard, he found that out one day.

Bo was a-slurpin' down a bowl of Rosie's Tuesday Lunchtime Special—tomater soup—when he laid his teeth on somethin' unexpected. It was hard as a bone! Now Bo, he scratched his head.

"Didn't think tomaters had bones," he muttered to himself.

He pulled that hard lump outta his mouth an' whaddya think he saw? Gold! A gold nugget the size of a bumblebee!

Bo gasped an' hid that nugget in his napkin, real quick-like.

"Soup too hot fer ya, Bo?" asked Tumbleweeze McPhearson from the next table.

"Huh—hot?" stuttered Bo. "It's fine, jest fine."

"Nobody makes tomater soup like Rosie," said Tumbleweeze, slurpin' up the last of his bowl. "Good as gold, if ya ask me."

"G-gold," stuttered old Bo, leanin' close over his soup. "You got that right!" Keepin' to himself, Bo dipped his fork in the soup an' stirred around like he was a-fishin'.

"Haw, haw," laughed out Tumbleweeze real sudden-like. Bo nearly jumped outta his skin.

"What you doin', Bo, eatin' soup with a fork? Haw, haw. I knows it's good an' thick when Rosie makes it. But a fork? Haw, haw!"

So Bo, he had to think quick, an' that was quite a challenge fer him. He sure didn't want to draw no 'ttention to himself. "Oh, that's jest what I was testin', uh, it's—uh, not quite as thick as usual."

So Tumbleweeze, he grabbed that fork outta Bo's fingers an' he tested it himself.

Bo was a-sweatin'.

"You're right, Bo," said the weasel. "It ain't as thick as mine was. Looks like it's been watered down!" Soup was drippin' offa the fork.

"Oh, no, uh—it's jest fine!" said Bo.

"Hey, Rosie," called out 'Weeze, "when'd you start waterin' down yer tomater soup?"

"Waterin' down?" said Rosie, lookin' surprised. "I don't water down no soup!"

"It's good soup, Miss Rosie, real gold—er good!" chimed in Bo. "There ain't no problem."

"I'll give ya a new bowl," said Rosie, "on the house." Then she called back to the kitchen, "Claude! Dish up a new bowl of tomater soup fer Bo here."

Well, Bo, he tried, but there weren't no stoppin' Rosie when she was tryin' to satisfy a customer. She came over an' tested that bowl of soup herself—an' she weren't too happy. Bo was afraid she came across another lump.

"This *is* watered down!" said Rosie.

"Told ye so," muttered Tumbleweeze.

Meanwhile, out came Claude, the kitchen help. "Sorry Miss Rosie, we's plumb outta yer tomater soup. I even had to stretch it a little towards the end."

Well, Rosie, she nearly had a tantrum. She stomped over to Claude an' said, "You watered this down! Why didn't you tell me we were runnin' out? I woulda mixed up another batch!"

Then she came back to Bo an' apologized. "Next time you come in, Bo, order anythin' you want—all on the house."

She shot a glare in Claude's direction. Claude slunk back inta the kitchen like a whipped coyote. "You still want the rest of that watered-down soup?" asked Rosie.

"Oh, yes!" said Bo, real eager. "The whole pan—er, bowl!"

"There'll be no charge fer that then," said Rosie, tearin' up Bo's check. Then she stomped back inta the kitchen to deal with Claude.

Well, the rest of old Bo's meal was perty quiet. An' he didn't find any more nuggets in that thar tomater soup. But he sure was a-wonderin' where that one piece of gold did come from. Then like a flash of lightnin' it came to him—it musta been from the water! So after things calmed down in the kitchen, Bo snuck back to talk to Claude himself.

"I was jest wonderin'," said Bo, "where'd that water come from that ya added inta the soup?"

"I's sorry," said Claude, "but ya ordered the special right at the end of lunchtime, an' I didn't have a full bowl left to serve, so I jest grabbed that bucket an' topped it off. T'weren't right." Claude hung his head low.

"No problem," said Bo, tryin' not to seem too curious. "But, uh, where's the bucket?"

"The bucket?" Claude scratched his head. "Thar in the corner. Why?"

"Oh—uh, seemed like that water had, uh, gold—er, good flavor," replied Bo, saunterin' over to the corner. He swished his hand around, lookin' real close-like. "Where'd ya git it?"

"Sheriff J.D. brings a bucket every day," answered Claude. "Don't know where he gets it. Guess you'll have to ask him."

So Bo, he headed right over to the sheriff's office quicker than a tumbleweed in a dust storm. He figured that if he could find where that water came from, he could start pannin' fer gold! An' when a feller found gold, he knew to gather it up quick—'cause word traveled fast in Dust River Gulch.

Well, wouldn't ya know it, Sheriff J.D. wasn't in. No sign of him nowhere. So Bo started askin' 'round, "Ya seen J.D.?" But nobody had.

He asked at the general store an' at the post office. Nope. He asked at the barber shop an' at the hotel. Nobody had seen him lately. 'Course when a feller went all 'round town askin' fer the sheriff—it stirred up some curiosity.

"What's the problem?" said Tumbleweeze, lookin' mighty curious. "Got some trouble?"

"No, no trouble," said Bo. "Jest lookin' fer J.D." He reached down into his pocket to feel the gold nugget. He sure didn't want to stir things up till he had a chance to do some pannin' fer himself. He strolled back toward home.

"Howdy, Bo!" called a familiar voice. "Heard you were a-lookin' fer me." An' wouldn't ya know it, there was Sheriff J.D. Saddlesoap, himself.

"Uh, sure am," Bo scratched his chin. He tried to act real casual an' calm, but his heart was beatin' like a thunderin' herd of cattle. "Jest a-wonderin', uh, where ya git yer water . . ."

J.D. looked mighty puzzled.

Bo kept on. "Ya know, the water ya git fer Rosie's restaurant every mornin'. Jest wonderin' where ya git it."

"You mean you been askin' all over town fer me, jest so you kin ask where I git water fer Rosie?" asked J.D., lookin' mighty curious.

Bo wiped some sweat offa his forehead, an' he looked down at his toes. "Yeah, guess that's 'bout it."

"From the creek out backa my house, Bo. Is there somethin' wrong with it?"

"Oh no, no—uh, it's fine water, gold—er, good water, J.D. Not a thing wrong with it, no siree. Gooood water. Mighty good water!"

Well, J.D. jest cocked his head an' looked at that old lizard kinda sideways.

Old Bo, he rubbed his chin an' said real casual-like, "Guess I'll be seein' ya, J.D." An' he turned an' sauntered back home.

Bo figured he better wait till dark to go pannin'. He sure didn't wanna start no gold rush. No sense gittin' people's curiosity up by wadin' 'round in broad daylight.

Well, it got dark a mite sooner than usual that night with some clouds rollin' in from the west. But it seemed like the afternoon lasted forever to old Bo. He was figurin' how he was gonna spend all that gold—once he got it.

He'd buy himself a fine new ten-gallon hat, or maybe a twenty- or thirty-gallon hat. He'd strut 'round town wearin' fancy clothes, imported from Kansas City! Why he'd be the talk of the town, he would!

He held the gold nugget in his hand an' told it, "Yer jest the first, Mr. Nugget. Tonight I pan out all yer glitterin' brothers an' sisters! Ha, ha!"

Well, finally it got dark an' quiet 'round town. Old Bo snuck out to the creek backa J.D.'s place. He kept his lamp low on the banks an' waded inta the gently-ripplin' water. Then he commenced his pannin' fer gold. He swished an' swashed one bucket after another. No gold yet.

He swished an' swashed some more, an' it started to rain. First it rained in drips an' droplets. Bo jest kept on pannin' there in the middle of that creek.

Then the rain came pourin'. It was a regular stampede of raindrops. Old Bo, he kept pannin'. No rainstorm was 'bout to keep him from strikin' it rich.

Then Bo heard a loud gurgling noise. He mighta thought it were the ocean, 'cept he hadn't never heard that. He looked up from his pannin' to see a wall of water rushin' down the creekbed. An' it was headed right fer him! He jumped up an' tried to slosh his way toward the bank.

"Help!" he yelled out.

Lucky fer him, J.D. heard that call. The sheriff jumped outta bed and looked out his back winder. He saw Bo's dim lantern flowin' downstream in the flood.

"Help!" cried Bo, tryin' to swim in the flood. But it weren't no use. He couldn't nearly reach the bank. That old lizard was bein' spun 'round (in that current) like a bug on a lasso.

Well, J.D. came at a gallop. He roped that half-drowned lizard by the tail an' pulled him back to the muddy shore.

"Bo! What you doin' in that creek at night—in the middle of a flash flood? Are you crazy?"

Bo hung his head. "Lookin' fer somethin'."

"Lookin' fer what—Davy Jones' locker? Yer lucky you weren't drowned!"

"I was lookin' fer gold."

"What?"

"Gold!"

"GOLD?" shouted J.D. "There ain't been no gold in that creek since my granddaddy panned fer it years ago."

"Somebody say gold?" yelled one neighbor from his winder.

"Gold!" came a cry from another cabin down the road.

An' perty soon 'most everbody in Dust River Gulch was comin' outta their houses with lanterns lit an' all sorts of pans, buckets, even a teapot or two. Folks were pannin' out by the rushin' creekbanks, some wearin' pajamas an' others in longjohns. It was a gold rush like you never seen.

In all that confusion, J.D. gave up tryin' to keep order. A-shakin' his head, he sauntered back to his house. Old Bo shuffled 'long beside him, his head hangin' down.

J.D. finally said, "Bo, why'd you figger there was gold in that thar creek?"

Bo pulled his one gold nugget outta his pocket. " 'Cause I thought this here come from the creek."

"Where'd you come up with it?" said J.D., studyin' that nugget real close-like.

"In Rosie's tomater soup."

"Tomater soup?" said J.D. dryin' out one ear. "Did you say tomater soup?"

"Tomater soup . . . thinned down with water from that bucket you took to Rosie's this mornin'." Bo rubbed his chin.

"That's why I asked ya where ya got that water. Figgered there'd be more where that come from."

Well, J.D. he scratched his head. Then he patted the pocket on the front of his shirt. He pulled that pocket out as fer as he could an' looked down inside. He started a-smilin', an' then laughin' an' a-snickerin'.

"What ya laughin' fer, J.D?"

"Bo, I wanna thank ya fer findin' my gold nugget!" He took the little chunk of gold from Bo's hand and held it up. "This here's my reward fer bringin' in Cactus-Face Curt. Jest got it yesterday. Put it in my shirt pocket." The sheriff started laughin' again.

"What happened?" asked Bo.

"Musta fallen outta my shirt pocket an' plopped right inta Rosie's bucket when I dipped up her water this mornin'!" J.D. jest laughed an' laughed. "Here, Bo, you keep it fer yer trouble!"

By dawn, the last of the gold panners at the creek had trudged back home in their drippin'-wet longjohns. Nobody found no gold, of course, since there wern't none there to be found. But nobody ever forgot the famous midnight gold rush of Dust River Gulch. Specially not old Bo, the lizard. Every Tuesday after that he went to Rosie's Restaurant for lunch, and sure 'nuff, he ordered tomater soup.

CHAPTER 4

Doc Hardly

Now fer a town full of critters, there wasn't no place more friendly to strangers than Dust River Gulch. An' we got our share of 'em—some stranger than others. Durin' busy times, we got two, maybe three strangers a week passin' through town. Don't figger any one of 'em felt more to home any-where else than they did right here—in the ol' Gulch town.

One of those more unfergettable strangers was that medicine-man that come through last spring. My, he had the town all astir, he did. He was a sleek-lookin' coyote with bushy gray sideburns. Called himself Doc Hardly.

"Get yer all-purpose imported moonbeam-elixir right here," he called out. "It'll cure what ails a body!"

An' that coyote, he looked over those town folks gathered 'round with more compassion than a cacklin' mother hen herself. "How 'bout you, neighbor? Has yer 'get-up-an'-go' done got up an' went? Has that spring in yer step turned to fall? Let me commend to you this fine elixir. On sale today fer the ground-scrapin' price of merely two dollars a bottle!"

Ol' Bo the lizard, he rubbed his chin.

Doc Hardly turned to him an' said, "You look a mite tired, neighbor. Kin I interest you in a good night's sleep? Rather, in the best night's sleep you done had since you were a little tike a-nappin' on yer dear mama's lap?" An' he held up a bottle of his elixir.

Bo sniffed a little an' pulled out two dollars right then an' there. "Give me a bottle of that thar elixir," he said. "I sure could use a rest like that!"

"I guarantee it, neighbor," said Doc. "Ya see, every bottle of this all-purpose imported moonbeam-elixir is absolutely, positivily, one hunderd an' ten percent guaranteed—er yer money back."

Another couple of fellers pulled out their money fer some elixir. "Good health to you, neighbors!" said Doc. "Would ya like to know the secret of this powerful-good elixir, neighbors?"

Folks nodded or shrugged. "Sure would," said somebody.

Well, Doc Hardly took a deep breath an' commenced his scientifical explainin'. "This elixir you see here in my hand draws its natural healin' power from the light of the moon! Why, every sailor on the seven seas knows the pull of the moonlight on the tides of the mighty seas is a force to be reckoned with. An' what do ya know? That same moonbeam power has been bottled up in this here elixir!"

That coyote took another deep breath, stared out over the prairie, an' commenced again. "In the far-away tropicorn islands near the equator, whar the sun shines hotter than a blacksmith's stove, an' the moon hangs low in the sky—nearly scrapin' the treetops—this powerful all-purpose elixir was made. Made at night, by the blazin' light of that tree-scrapin' moon. This moonbeam-elixir catches that natural moonbeam power an' traps it in this here bottle ya see before ya today!"

By this time, a couple more townsfolk were pullin' out two dollars fer their own bottle of Doc Hardly's elixir.

"Good health to ya, neighbors!" said Doc. "Take a couple of swallers 'fore bedtime tonight. Tomorrow mornin' you'll wake up feelin' fresher than a tadpole!"

Then Doc Hardly, he stopped a minute, an' hung down his head an' stroked his bushy sideburns. "I got to tell you kind folks," he said, "though it'll cut into my earnings severe-like, that this all-purpose imported moonbeam-elixir does have a fault. Once ya open that bottle-top, its moonbeam-power don't last long atall. But I've found myself a way to recharge it, so ya don't have to buy a new bottle every few days."

Well, Dust River Gulch folks, they did apperciate sech honesty. I figger it made the most suspicious of 'em feel a good bit kinder towards this stranger.

"How d'ya recharge it, Doc?" asked Bo.

"Well, good neighbor," said Doc, "I leave my open bottle on the windersill overnight, with my winder wide open. That way it kin soak up new moonbeam-power whiles I'm a-dreamin' of those moon-soaked beaches of the tropicorn islands."

"Soun's easy 'nuff," snorted Bo.

"Jest make sure yer winder's wide open, neighbor, so those moonbeams kin come in full-power," said the coyote, with the most friendly-some smile you ever seen.

"Thankee kindly," said Bo.

Then one burly mountain-goat snorted out, "Bo, yer the feller that done struck it rich in that 'gold rush.' You kin afford a new bottle anyways!" An' several town folks snickered an' poked at each other. (Of course, you recall that story, I'm sure.)

Old Bo, he frowned an' snorted a bit. Folks don't ferget too quick in Dust River Gulch. An' he sauntered back home, while Doc Hardly commenced talkin' again.

That night, Bo took two swallers of that all-purpose imported moonbeam-elixir. Then he put it on his windersill, bein' careful to see that his winder was wide open, jest like Doc said. An' he hopped inta bed, a-thinkin' 'bout those perty-soundin' tropicorn islands.

Now don't ya know that when Bo woke up next mornin' he felt like a new lizard! He hadn't never felt more rested!

"Better go cap up that moonbeam-elixir," he said to himself. "Sure don't wanna waste it!" He went to the winder an' squinted his eyes. "Awful bright already." Bo poked his head out to see the clock on the post office down the street.

"Nine-thirty!" he yelped. "I cain't recall last time I slept that late!"

So Bo went to throw on his pants, an' he patted against his pocket. "Hey, whar is it?" he asked himself. "Whar's my gold nugget? It's gone!"

Well, 'fore ya know it, Bo went a-runnin' down the street. There was already a bunch of townsfolk gathered 'round Doc Hardly, who was tryin' to sell his elixir again.

"What's a matter, Bo?" asked somebody.

"Didn't that elixir do ya right?" asked a mountain goat.

"It ain't the elixir," said Bo. "I been robbed!"

"Robbed?" said several folks together.

"Took my gold nugget, my wallet, even the pocketwatch my old granddaddy gave me. It's all been stole!"

"I'll go git J.D.!" said Tumbleweeze, an' off he went to Rosie's Restaurant.

"Good neighbor!" said Doc Hardly, who'd nearly been fergotten in the confusion. "It grieves me considerable, to have one of my fine customers treated so! I cain't do much to fix it, but kin I at least offer ya another half dozen bottles of this fine elixir? At no cost, of course."

"Thankee kindly," said Bo. He pulled out his hankie an' blew his nose. "That's mighty kind of ya. It were mighty good elixir, Doc."

"I'm so glad to hear that, neighbor," said the coyote. He put his arm 'round Old Bo there in fronta those town folks gathered 'round. "Tell me—tell all of us, how did ya sleep last night after takin' a helpin' of this all-purpose imported moonbeam-elixir?"

"Like a baby, Doc," said Bo. "Ain't never slept better!"

Doc, he patted Old Bo on the shoulder an' said, "Glad to be of service to ya, neighbor. Though it pains me to know of yer misfortune, I'm glad that at least, after the toils an' troubles of the day, you kin look forward to a peaceable night's sleep."

Then he looked out to all those town folks with more compassion than a she-bear lookin' after her cubs, an' said, "That's all I wants fer any an' all of ya. Fer you kind, hard-workin' folks—I'm gonna cut my profits to the bone, an' offer you this powerful-good all-purpose imported moonbeam-elixir fer the self-sacrificin' price of only one an' a half dollars a bottle. You deserve it, good neighbors, just like Bo here."

Well, that elixir started selling fast! Most everbody gathered 'round bought one or two bottles apiece. An' Bo, he was helpin' Doc Hardly pass it out.

"An' remember," said Doc. "To make it last, leave the open bottle in yer open windersill tonight. Let those moonbeams recharge it fer ya! Got a full moon comin' tonight!"

"Ain't that somethin'?" said Bo.

"Guess I came to town at the right time," said Doc, sellin' one bottle of elixir after another.

'Bout this time, Sheriff J.D. trotted up to the gatherin'.

"J.D.!" said Bo. "Tumbleweeze tell ya? I been robbed!"

"Yep!" said J.D. "C'mon over to my office. We'll track down the crim'nal!"

"Best of luck to ya, Sheriff!" called out Doc Hardly, real sincere-like.

"Thankee," said J.D., "but I don't believe we has met before. I'm the sheriff 'round these parts, Sheriff J.D. Saddlesoap."

"Doc Hardly," said the coyote with a tip of his hat, "at yer service."

"What ya sellin' here, Mr. Hardly?" asked J.D.

"Jest call me Doc," said the coyote. "An' I'm so glad ya asked, Sheriff! This here product is what every hard-workin', law-abidin' citizen needs, come the end of the day. It's a cure fer what ails a body. It's my all-purpose imported moonbeam-elixir. An' it'll give a feller the most relaxin' night's sleep he done ever had! But you kin ask our friend Bo 'bout that."

"He's got that right; ain't never slept better! " said Bo. "Here ya go, J.D. Have yerself a bottle—my treat."

"Now there's a good neighbor fer ya!" called out Doc Hardly. "What better gift kin ya give, than the gift of good health! Good health to ya, Sheriff! An' I hopes ya has a powerful-good night's sleep to boot."

"Thankee," said J.D., though he looked a mite distracted. Then he an' Bo headed on back to the office. An' Doc Hardly, he kept sellin' that moonbeam-elixir better'n ever.

Don't suppose thar's much news 'bout that afternoon, 'cept that J.D. didn't find nothin' 'bout who stole Bo's goods—not a clue! An' Doc Hardly, he musta sold outta that elixir of his. It was more pop'lar than the Tuesday Special at Rosie's.

Well 'fore ya know it, the sun set over the hills west of Dust River Gulch an' the full moon came risin' in the east. It were a mighty quiet night in the old Gulch town—powerful-quiet! Course, in nearly every open winder in town, there was a bottle of rechargin' moonbeam-elixir. Even J.D.'s windersill had a bottle. Seemed like the whole town been swept away to those dreamy tropicorn islands!

But who do ya think was still up an' about the town? None other than Doc Hardly himself! There he was, walkin' down the street at midnight, a-headin' fer an open winder. He slithered right inta Cyrus Skunk's bedroom, poked 'round a bit inside, real quiet-like, an' popped back out again, a-headin' fer another open winder!

Well, this mighta gone on fer a good while, 'cept fer an interruption.

"Evenin' Doc!" called out someone just come from 'round the corner.

Now it was kinda dark to tell fer sure, but it seemed like that coyote jumped back a space 'fore he replied, calm as kin be, "Why good evenin', Sheriff!"

"Out kinda late, aren'tcha?" asked J.D.

"Oh, uh, guess I am, now that ya mentioned it," said Doc. "An' you too, eh, Sheriff?"

"Jest couldn't sleep," said J.D.

"Why that's a pity, Sheriff. I thought our good friend Bo gave you a bottle of my elixir."

"Yep, he did."

"Thought I saw an open bottle in yer windersill," said the Doc, 'fore he thought better of it.

"Now that's a good ways from here," said J.D., raisin' one eyebrow. "Guess you been walkin' 'round a while. You ain't havin' trouble sleepin', are ya?"

"Well, uh, matter a fact I am," said the coyote, "Done sold outta my elixir! Didn't leave none fer myself! Ain't that a predicament?"

"Could be," said J.D., "except I might be able to help. Ya see, Bo, he gave me a couple extra bottles of his. An' I got 'em right here with me." J.D. pulled out a bottle from each of his vest pockets. "One fer you, an' one fer me. Here ya go, Doc!"

"Oh, uh, thankee kindly, Sheriff. Yer too generous!"

"Aw, ain't nothin', Doc, specially after all yer kindness an' concern fer everbody here." J.D., he opened up his bottle of elixir an' took a swig, "C'mon, Doc, we'll walk together till the sleepiness comes on."

"Oh, uh, sure 'nuff, Sheriff," said Doc, takin' the tiniest swaller of his moonbeam-elixir.

J.D., he scratched his mane. He looked Doc Hardly square in the eye an' said, "Ya know, I think I knows the problem here, Doc. Why—we ain't takin' 'nuff of this here elixir!"

"Oh, really?"

"Of course, that's got to be it! Yer a medicine-man yerself—see if'n ya figger I'm right. I'm a sorta big, horsey feller. I needs more elixir to do the trick—more than some little feller like say Bo the lizard needs, right?"

Well that coyote, he perks up an' said, "I believe yer right, Sheriff! Go right ahead an' drink the whole bottle."

"Ya think so?"

"Sure," said Doc.

Then J.D., he swallered down that whole bottle of elixir, wiped his mouth, an' said with a smile, "Doctor's orders."

Doc Hardly, he smiled an' shakes his head, "Ya know all these years I been perscribin' this elixir, an' I ain't never thought of that, Sheriff. But ya know what they say, 'the bigger they is, the harder they falls—asleep that is!'"

J.D., he laughed with Doc, an' they commenced walkin' down the street together. But 'fore long, J.D. blurted out, "How about you, Doc? Ain't you gonna have no more?"

Doc said, "Well, now, I ain't as big as you, Sheriff. Don't wanna take too much."

J.D., he scratched his mane again. "I been thinkin' here, Doc. You been takin' this elixir yerself fer quite some time, ain't ya?"

"Well, sure, uh, as needs be."

"Yer body has plumb gotten used to it, Doc. Ya needs to up yer dosage!"

At that, J.D. pulled the bottle right outta Doc Hardly's paw, an' put it up to that coyote's lips. "Go ahead, Doc, take a few swallers more."

Doc, he took a tiny swaller or two.

"Naw," said J.D., tippin' up the bottle. "Ya need more'n that!" An' that wide-eyed coyote done swallered more'n half that bottle 'fore J.D. let go of it.

"Sheriff's orders!" laughed J.D.

Well, those two commenced walkin' down that moonlit street. J.D. was a-talkin' an' laughin' an' tellin' jokes. But Doc Hardly, he was perty quiet. In fact, he got quieter an' quieter. His feet started a-shufflin', steppin' slower an' slower. An' wouldn't ya know it—he plumb fell asleep on his feet, a-leanin' against J.D.!

Next mornin' ol' Bo came over to J.D.'s office an' what did he hear? Snorin', powerful-snorin' that was louder'n a sawmill! "J.D.?" he called out. "You here?"

J.D., he sprang out from the back room. "Mornin', Bo," he said. But that terrible snorin' didn't quit. J.D. reached down in his pocket an' pulled out Bo's wallet, his gold nugget, an' that pocketwatch. "Believe these is yers," said J.D.

"Whar'd ya git those?" yelped Bo, nearly beside himself.

"From that feller I got locked up in the back," said J.D.

"Ya mean that snorin' feller's the thief?"

"Yep—Doc Hardly. He won't be sellin' no more sleepin' potion fer a long time," said J.D. "Perty clever trick though: put the town to sleep with their winders open, then go 'round an' steal 'em blind at night." J.D. picked up an elixir bottle from his desk an' took a few swallers.

Bo, he cocked his head. "Why you still drinkin' that stuff then—in the mornin' yet?"

J.D., he threw back his head an' laughed. "This?" he said. "I poured that potion outta this bottle right after you gave it to me yesterday. Jest been fillin' it with soda water since. Handy bottles, ain't they? An' they still look like the real thing."

CHAPTER 5

Hare-Raisin' Horseshoes

There ain't nothin' more irritatin' than losin' somethin' that ya needs real bad, like yer shoes, or worse yet—yer reputation! A while back, our very own J.D. Saddlesoap, a thoroughbred sheriff with as fine a pedigree as you ever seen, got inta such a fix! 'Course it didn't happen all at once. First off it was his shoes what come up missin'. An' we'll git to the part 'bout his reputation directly.

There weren't hardly a soul with better organiziniz, oregoniz . . . what I mean to say is, J.D., he kept things in order. Perty good skill to have fer a lawman. So one mornin' when his shoes came up a-missin'—well, he was mighty puzzled.

He was a-lookin' under his stove fer those shoes, when who should show up to the door? Well, it was Miss Rosie. She was wearin' her apron, an' lookin' pertier than a pichure painted in Paris, France.

She called out, sweet as honey, "I brought ya a sweet roll fer breakfast, J.D." 'Course they had been courtin' fer some time by now. It wasn't long after that matter with Gruffle O'Buffalo an' his gang of bum steers when they got started.

"Why, Rosie, thank ya kindly," said J.D., rubbin' at some soot on his nose. "Ain't nothin' sweeter than yer sweet rolls, specially when ya deliver 'em yerself."

Rosie, she turned sorta pinkish, an' it seemed like there was a sparkle in her eye. "Yer more than welcome, J.D." Then she asked, "What ya lookin' fer down there?"

"Well, ya won't hardly believe it, Rosie," said J.D., "but I cain't find my shoes."

"Oh, dear," said Rosie, with genuine concern.

"Thought I left 'em on the doorstep, jest like always," said J.D.

"Don't figger anybody'd steal 'em, do ya?" asked Rosie.

"Cain't see why they'd want to—got my initials on 'em." said J.D. "Besides, they were gittin' kinda worn anyways."

"Why don'tcha stop by the smith an' git yerself a new pair then," said Rosie. "Put it on my bill. It kin be an early birthday present fer ya."

"Why, Rosie, that's mighty sweet of ya," said J.D. "Kin I walk ya back to town? If'n, that is, ya don't mind my bare feet on the way."

"Why it'd be my pleasure," she said. "With shoes, or without 'em." An' off to town they went.

'Course that wasn't the end of the matter concernin' those lost shoes, but we still got the matter of that lost reputation to explain. Now to lose a reputation is a mite harder than jest losin' a set of horseshoes, specially when ya been 'round as long as J.D. Cain't think of any law-abidin' folks what didn't respect him, 'cept fer maybe Hare-Brain Jack.

You may not be acquainted with Hare-Brain Jack. He ain't been 'round these parts long. Rumor has it that Jack used to run a barbershop back east. But he didn't talk much about it. Fact is, that jackrabbit didn't talk much 'bout anythin'. Kept to himself most times. Hotheaded as a Texas gila monster, though. Ya sure didn't want to cross him. Seemed like he was gonna start up a shop here in Dust River Gulch. That's how he an' J.D. had their fallin' out.

If I recall correctly, J.D. offered to be Jack's first customer. But after that haircut, J.D. revoked his license to operate. Seemed like perty harsh treatment. 'Course you could say the same fer that haircut too. J.D. wore his hat everwhere fer nearly two months.

Jack got inta farmin' after that. Strange feller, though. Swung that hoe like an Injun warrior. Young'ns, I 'magine that's why yer mamas don't let ya play near Hare-Brain's place.

Anyways, Hare-Brain Jack, he was mad as a cornered hornet! Ya see, somebody done trampled his prize carrot garden—stomped right through it! He done studied those footprints, an' what do ya think he saw? They were horseshoe prints—with initials—none other than—you guessed it—J.D.!

Well, Jack, he came stompin' up the main street, a-stirrin' up the dust, an' yellin' fer the sheriff like his life depended on it. Or somebody's life, anyways.

"I's gonna scalp that low-down excuse fer a sheriff! If'n he thinks he kin stomp through my property like he owns it himself—I'll show him real justice! Maybe he thinks he owns this ol' Gulch town. Well he ain't dealt with the likes of Hare-Brain Jack!"

'Course them words stirred up a peck of curiosity from all the folks in town. They couldn't hardly imagine such a thing, not from J.D.!

Jest then J.D. himself stepped outta the smith's shop, wearin' his brand-new shiney horseshoes.

"Thar's the culprit!" yelled out that half-crazed jackrabbit. An' he rushed towards J.D. like a chargin' bull. He stopped no more'n one inch away from J.D.'s puzzled-lookin' face an' blasted out like a duststorm. "You done it! Ya thinks that changin' yer shoes was good enough to cover fer yer trespassin' footprints on my best carrot patch! Well, Mr. J.D. 'Shoeprint' Saddlesoap, it ain't gonna be that easy! Yer initials are all over my garden!"

"What you talkin' 'bout, Jack?" asked J.D.

"Don't you deny it, Sheriff! Ya stomped all over my carrot garden! Ya trampled my best carrots! An' that badge ain't gonna git ya outta this either. My cousin Harry is a Philadelphia lawyer, an' he kin help me prove it in a court of law. That's if'n I don't deal with ya first—my own way."

'Bout this time, Rosie came thatta way an' asked, "What's goin' on here?"

"Ain't none of yer business ma'am," yelled Hare-Brain Jack.

"If ya don't quit yer yellin' at J.D., yer gonna be wearing this iron skillet on yer head, Jack," said Rosie, calm as anythin'.

"She ain't jest a-whistlin' Dixie," called out Claude, Rosie's kitchen help at the restaurant. 'Course that raised a few snickers in the crowd. Everbody knew ya didn't mess with Rosie, specially Claude.

Jack quieted down some, but he still looked plenty mad. "Mr. J.D. here done trampled all over my carrot garden. Left his initials all over it. An' he ain't gonna git away with it."

"Why don't we jest go down an' see fer ourselves," said Rosie. An' so they did.

Perty near the whole town walked down to Hare-Brain Jack's to look over the damage. It was considerable too. It weren't like those hoofprints were jest a-passin' through that carrot patch. They were stamped all over the place! An' everwhere ya looked, ya saw them initials—J.D.!

Now the town folks didn't know what to make of it. They couldn't hardly imagine J.D. doin' sech a thing, but there were all them "J.D."s pressed inta that soft dirt. What else were they to think?

J.D., he looked at Rosie. An' Rosie she looked at J.D., along with most everbody else.

"Well, that explains that," said J.D.

" 'Splains what?" said Hare-Brain Jack.

"Somebody done stole my shoes after all," said J.D.

"Ah, c'mon, Sheriff," Jack scoffed. "D'ya expect me to believe some cockamamie excuse like that?"

"J.D. was just lookin' fer 'em this morning," said Rosie. "Jest when I stopped by."

"Yer sayin' somebody else done stole yer shoes, put 'em on, an' came out to trample my carrot patch?" Jack sneered somethin' fierce an' shook his head. "From the look of these prints, it'd have to be some other horse 'bout yer size that done it. Look how they're spaced out. Cain't think of no other horse yer size in Dust River Gulch!"

"There's Ol' Gray Marey," said Tumbleweeze 'fore he thought much 'bout it. " 'Course she ain't what she used to be."

"She couldn't an' she wouldn't," said J.D.

"An' there's Ro—" Claude stopped himself, whiles nearly everbody gave him a stare cold 'nuff to freeze out a campfire. The whole town knew Rosie wouldn't even think of such a thing.

"How 'bout that outlaw, Trigger McGee?" asked Ol' Bo.

"Naw," said J.D. "He an' his gal Molly been sent up to the state prison. Saw to that myself."

"Well, then," sneered Hare-Brain Jack, "that jest leaves you, don't it, Sheriff? An' everbody here knows we's had our fallin' out."

Well, it were mighty quiet thar by that trampled carrot patch. Ya could almost hear those drops of sweat fallin' offa J.D.'s face. Finally he said, "Gimme one week, Jack, an' I'll git to the bottom of this."

Hare-Brain Jack, he squinted his eyes an' scratched his long skinny ears. "All right, Sheriff. Ya got one week. But then there's gonna be a scalpin' fer the scoundrel what done this, if'n I have anythin' to say about it!"

So everbody started a-shufflin' back to their business. They were a-shakin' their heads an' mumblin' to each other. Hardly nobody dared look J.D. in the eye as they left him standin' there. Rosie, she put her hoof on his shoulder an' said, "C'mon J.D., let's go on back to the restaurant."

But 'fore he did, J.D. took one step inta the soft dirt at the edge of that garden. An' he noticed somethin' perty unusual. His hoofprints were sunk down way deeper than any of the others in that carrot patch. "Now ain't that curious?" he said to himself.

"I'd apperciate it," said the jackrabbit, real mean-like, "if'n ya'd git yer trespassin' hooves offa my property!"

"Kin I help fix yer garden up?" asked J.D.

"No thank ya, Sheriff! You done 'fixed' it up enough already!" said Jack. "Now if'n you'll excuse yerselves, I got to see if'n I kin salvage some carrots." An' with that, ol' Hare-Brain commenced tearing inta that garden, swingin' his hoe like it was a tomahawk.

As they were leavin', J.D. whispered, "I think I got an idear, Rosie."

Next mornin' J.D. was puttin' up paper announcements all over town. Tumbleweeze McPhearson was a-gulpin' down his breakfast grits over at Rosie's place when J.D. came in, tacked one on the wall, an' went on his way. Well, you kin imagine it weren't but two seconds 'fore Tumbleweeze was over there, readin' that announcement to everbody in the place. Folks in Dust River Gulch, they tend to depend on ol' Tumbleweeze fer their news, an' of course, he don't mind the tellin'.

So the weasel clears his throat of grits, an' reads out loud an' clear:

HORSESHOE-PLAYIN' CHAMPEENSHIP!
THIS COMIN' SATURDAY ON MAIN STREET
ALL COMERS IS WELCOME TO PLAY
SURPRISE FER THE WINNER!

Well, that really stirred things up at Rosie's. First off, horseshoes was perty important to folks in the old Gulch town. Not jest fer wearin', but fer playin'. (Fact is, any critter that didn't play horseshoes wasn't hardly worth his salt, 'cordin' to some folks, that is.) Second off, a body couldn't help but wonder why J.D. wasn't more busy with other things.

"Why ain't J.D. spendin' his time lookin' fer that carrot-garden trampler?" asked Bo the lizard.

"Maybe he didn't need to find him," said a burly mountain goat by the door. "Maybe he done that tramplin' himself after all."

Now that thar comment by the goat brought everthing to the boilin' point at Rosie's place. There was considerable fussin' an' fumin'. Bo gave thought to punchin' that critter right in the nose. But he thunk better. Other fellers started a-shoutin' at each other. Some were a-rollin' up their sleeves. Ya see thar was quite a difference of opinion regardin' the guilt or innocence of Sheriff J.D. Saddlesoap.

"'Course he done it," yelled one longhorn steer across the room.

"No way!" yelled another feller.

An' so it went, till Rosie, she stomped out from the kitchen. "Y'all hush up!" she said. "I don't wanna hear one more word 'bout J.D. an' Hare-Brain Jack till this thing's resolved next week! Everbody understand that?"

Well that longhorn, he mumbled somethin' 'bout J.D. under his breath. But don't you know, Rosie, she heard it. She stomped right over to that big steer's table without sayin' a word. She yanked that feller up outta his seat by his left ear, an' she pulled him outta her front door. All the time that steer's a-whimperin' like a calf who's lost his mama.

When the door slammed behind her, Rosie stood there a-lookin' over everbody else. An' it were mighty quiet in that thar restaurant. Ya coulda heard a cactus quill drop. Rosie, she smiled real sweet-like an' asked, "Now, anybody intersted in this horseshoe champeenship a-comin' up?" An' wouldn't ya know it, everbody seemed real agreeable.

Come Saturday mornin', the main street was jest full of folks. 'Most every feller in town had signed up fer the champeenship, an' a few able-ladies too. Even a rattler showed up, all decked out like a real cowpoke. J.D., he hammered an iron stake at both ends of the dusty main street, an' the horseshoes started flyin'!

Clink.

"Ooooh."

Clank.

"Aaaaah."

Thud. An' there was a coupla chuckles from the crowd lookin' on.

Clod-dinga-ding.

"Ringer!" came up the shout.

Well, the competition was mighty intense. An' thar were so many folks signed up that it took mosta the day to narrow things down. Don't believe nobody went home, though. Like I said, horseshoes was perty important to folks in Dust River Gulch.

By the time the shadows were stretchin' out like stilts, the horseshoe playin' champeenship had done been whittled down to the two best players. It was the final round, winner take all! As you might expect, J.D. was one of 'em. An' the other one, to most everbody's surprise, was that unfamiliar-lookin' rattlesnake.

Now that rattler, he was dressed like a cowboy outta the Wild West Show or some such thang! Had a kerchief over his mouth, an' chaps on, er, jest one chap (of course, snakes don't have no legs). An' he had jest the peculiar-est way of tossin' horseshoes you ever seen! He'd pick one up with his rattlin' tail, an' spin it 'round an' 'round—why he'd make his body inta a regular lasso 'fore he'd let that shoe fly!

An' what a foller-through! It seemed like his tail'd stretch nearly half way to the opposite stake! That's probably why he was so stinkin' accurate. I never seen so many ringers as that rattler rung up!

Tumbleweeze McPhearson, he stepped inta the street an' said, "Alright, folks. This here's what y'all been waitin' fer—the horseshoe champeenship of Dust River Gulch!"

An' what a cheer come up from the crowd then!

"Our two finalists is—first, Sheriff J.D. Saddlesoap."

There were a good amount of cheerin' fer him, though not a clap from Hare-Brain Jack.

"An' second, the amazin' rattler." He got a thunderin' applause! He truly was amazin'.

"Hope he beats ya good, Sheriff!" said Jack to J.D.

"All I kin say is, may the best feller win," said J.D. An' he stepped over to shake the rattler's hand, or somethin' ('course, snakes don't have no hands).

An' the two commenced their horseshoe-playin'. First went the rattlesnake.

Whooptey, whooptey. 'Round he spun an' let 'er fly.
Clod-dinga, ding. Ringer, of course.

Then J.D. let one fly.

Clod-dinga-dinga, ding. A ringer fer J.D.

Whooptey, whooptey. Fling.

Clod-dinga, ding. Another ringer fer the rattler.

Clod-ding. Another fer J.D.

Well, believe it or not, this went on fer three rounds an' a half. Everyone a ringer! I ain't never seen J.D. play so good before. He sure wasn't losin' none of his shoes today. All ringers! An' the snake—well, don't believe he'd missed one all day!

It was the rattler's final toss of the game, now. He could finish up a perfect game if he made this one.

Whooptey, whooptey, whooooptey, whooooooooptey. He spun 'round like a tornado an' let that shoe fly! It flew higher'n than any of the others—way up, up, up—an' it flew

way over the stake on the other side. You wouldda thought thatta done it. But that horseshoe were still a-flyin'. It flew right 'round the flagpole at the post office way down the street, an' then—it looped back! Jest like a boomerang, it came screamin' back. Well, some folks ducked fer cover, let me tell ya! Back it came a-flyin'.

CLANG! Clod-dinga, dinga, dinga, dinga dinga, ding.

"A ringer!" yelled the crowd, an' they burst inta clappin' like a thundercloud.

An' that snake, he took himself a bow.

'Course, J.D., he was a mite shook-up. But he took his aim, swung forwards, an' let it fly.

Clink.

"Awwwww."

J.D. shook his head.

Tumbleweeze, he announced, "An' the champeen horse-shoe player of Dust River Gulch—the amazin' rattler!" Everbody cheered again. Specially Hare-Brain Jack.

Then J.D., he cleared his throat an' said, "I got to admit, I ain't never seen a better horseshoe player." An' he turned to his opponent an' said, "Before yer surprise, would ya be willin' to do a few more tossin' tricks fer the folks here?"

"Yeah. Let's see some more!" said lotsa folks.

The rattler, he nodded an' bowed. An' then he commenced.

First he did another boomerang shot—*Clod-dinga dinga, ding*. Then he took four shoes, all at once. He started a-jug-glin' 'em with his teeth an' tail. Then one by one, he flicked 'em over to the far stake. *Clod-ding. Clod-ding. Clod-ding. Clod-ding.*

Well, the folks went wild! They was a-clappin' an' a-hol-lerin', "Hooray!"

Then J.D. said, "I got a trick fer ya. 'Course it might be too hard fer ya . . . but kin ya take a shoe on each side an plant 'em right in my tracks whiles I trots ahead of ya?"

An' the crowd cheered, "Yeah, you kin do anythin'!"

An' 'fore J.D. even laid down tracks, that snake galloped up the street an' back. One shoe in his mouth an' the other on his tail. Funniest thing you ever saw! 'Course everbody was a-cheerin' an' laughin' like nobody's business.

But Sheriff J.D. Saddlesoap, he took off his shiny new shoes, with those "J.D." initials on 'em an' said to that snake, "Now, kin ya do the same thang with these shoes?" Then he glanced over to Hare-Brain, "Do *you* think he kin, Jack?"

Well, everbody got real quiet-like. An' the amazin' rattler stopped his struttin' an' tried to slither away. J.D. galloped over to him an yanked his kerchief down offa his face. "In fact, you already done it once before in a carrot patch, ain'tcha—Snake-Eye Smith?"

J.D. grabbed that rattler 'round the neck quicker than you could say "ringer," an he put him into handcuffs ('course snakes don't have no hands, so he put his head in one side an' his tail in the other). "Snake-Eye, yer under arrest, fer trespassin' an' fer impersonatin' a sheriff! Not to mention escapin' from the state prison."

Well, the town folks cheered louder than they had done all day. Several folks came over to pat J.D. on the back or shake his hoof. An' wouldn't ya know it, so did ol' Hare-Brain Jack, himself.

"Thank ya, Sheriff," he said. "An' I'm powerful sorry I caused all that trouble fer ya."

"That's all right," said J.D. "An' ya know what? I think if'n you don't try to open up yer barber shop again—we kin even be friends."

An' those two fellers, they had a good laugh together.

So what about that scalpin', ya say? Well, all I kin tell ya is Hare-Brain Jack has an awful big snakeskin hangin' up over his door nowadays. (Too bad snakes don't have no hair, ain't it, Snake-Eye?)

STILL at LARGE

GRUFFLE O'BUFFALO

AND

HIS GANG OF BUM STEERS

The Biggest, Baddest, Meanest, Mangiest
Herd of Outlaws West of the Mississippi!

CHAPTER 6
End of the Rodeo

Did ya ever notice how jest when ya thought ya had a problem licked, that here it would come back into yer face all over again? It was perty irritatin' wasn't it?—jest like tossin a bucket of water into a stiff wind.

Well, sometimes the folks here in Dust River Gulch plumb felt jest like that. Jest when we thought we'd seen the last of some lowdown, no account outlaw—whaddya know? He showed his face back in town again! Of course that was the way it was with Snake-Eye Smith. Seemed like that rattler could slither outta most any state prison! J.D. perty near lost his reputation when that sly ol' rattler came back, now didn't he?

But you could take Snake-Eye along with 'most all the ornriest outlaws west of the Mississippi—put 'em all together an' turn 'em loose on Dust River Gulch itself, an' you wouldn't be near as bad off as ya would with one particular outlaw on the loose. I 'magine ya know who I'm talkin' about.

J.D. was outta town, scoutin' fer a deputy, when folks got wind of trouble. Jest like last time, Tumbleweeze McPhearson sensed it a-comin'.

"What's that rumblin' noise?" he said.

"I don't hear nothin'," said Bo the lizard.

So the weasel, he put his ear down to the ground, right thar in the middle of the street. "Uh-oh," he said, an' his eyes got real big-like. Then he looked off over the prairie.

"What is it?" asked Bo.

Then they saw it—that cloud a dust all stirred up an' a-comin' this way.

"A tornader!" gasped Bo.

"Nope," said Tumbleweeze. "Worse'n that."

"Ya don't mean it," said the lizard, a-shakin' all over.

"Yep, they's back!"

Well, perty soon the whole town was stirred up jest like it *was* a tornader! Everbody scattered outta the street an' offa the boardwalks quicker than you kin finish sayin' "Gruffle O'Buffalo!" ('Course that was what everbody *was* sayin'.)

Yep, they were back—ol' Gruff an' his gang of bum steers. An' there were more of 'em this time. Anyways, they rumbled inta town, did their usual hootin' an' hollerin', an' then they headed inta Rosie's Restaurant. The steers, they set themselves down, takin' up a whole table by themselves.

Then in came two brahma bulls, black as coal, an' bigger than most any critters you've seen in these parts ('cept of course, ol' Gruffle himself).

That big mangy buffalo, he gave a snort an' swung open the doors there at Rosie's. An' he commenced his struttin' 'round the place. (You woulda thunk he were a king, wouldn't ya?)

"Howdy, folks," said Gruff, kinda sneerin'. "Good to see y'all again!"

'Course everbody at Rosie's was quiet as a field mouse. They all had their heads hung down low betweenst their shoulders, keepin' one eye on that struttin' buffalo.

Gruff kept on. "Ain't ya glad to see me an' my boys again?" That started them bum steers snickerin'. No feller in his right mind wouldda been glad to see that gang of outlaws, an' they all knew it.

Gruff sauntered over to those big bulls an' said, "Let me make yer acquaintance with Bully—"

One brahma-bull nodded his head an' gave a snort that pert-near shook the rafters.

"—An' his twin brother, Bully."

The other bull snorted an' *did* shake the rafters.

"They's a lot like their Brahma Mama—don't have much 'magination, an' mighty ornery to boot," said Gruff. "But I'm sure we'll all git along jest fine. Right boys?"

The bull-brothers jest snorted again, makin' 'most everbody in the place duck their heads fer the noise. An' them bum steers commenced a-snickerin' all over again.

"We's thirsty, gal!" Gruff yelled out in Rosie's direction. "Get a 'round of milkshakes fer my boys, here."

So Rosie, she got right to it, quick as Claude could stir-em up, she brought the shakes out to that mangy lot of outlaws. Then she said, "How 'bout you, Mr. Buffalo? Would ya care fer two, maybe three gallons of sour milk?" (That Rosie, she was mighty plucky, wasn't she?)

Gruffle, he raised himself up an' glared at Rosie somethin' fierce. "No ma'am," he growled. "Not this time! But that reminds me, I gots some unfinished business in town to tend to. Don't I boys?"

They were all busy slurpin' down their milkshakes, so Gruff said again, "DON'T I, BOYS?"

Well that made fer enough agreeable snorts from Gruff's gang to nearly shake a feller outta his cowboy boots.

"Last time I was here, seemed like me an' the sheriff were competin' in a rodeo," said Gruff. "But wouldn't ya know it—I took sick 'fore we was done."

Ya probably remember why that buffalo took sick, now don't ya? An' Rosie, she couldn't hardly keep from smilin' when she thought 'bout it.

Gruffle commenced speakin' again. "Well, this time all yer connivin' won't do the trick, gal. Ya jest tell yer dear Sheriff Saddlesoap to meet me at the Oakey-Dokey Corral outside of town at noon tomorra'. We's gonna finish up that rodeo competition—er my name ain't Gruffle O'Buffalo!"

Then the place shook with all kinds of hootin' an' hollerin' from that worthless gang of steers an' them two Bully brothers.

Gruff called out, "C'mon, boys," an' they stomped out to the door. Jest 'fore he stepped out, Gruff turned, reached inta his pocket, pulled out a handful of coins, set 'em on the counter, an' smiled real big. "Almost fergot, ma'am. Nearly left without payin'! Cain't have that, now can we?" An' those bum steers started some fearsome snickerin'. "Don't you ferget to tell that sheriff—I'll see him tomorra' at the Oakey-Dokey Corral!" An' with that they were gone a-rumblin' down the main street, hootin' an' hollerin' like a barnyard at chowtime.

Well, J.D. came back that night. He hadn't been able to find no deputy nowhere. An' when he found out that Gruffle O'Buffalo an' his gang were back in town, it didn't make him feel better. He sure could've used some help dealin' with that collection of crim'nals! Of course, when he heard 'bout the rodeo competition, he weren't exactly as happy as a dog with two tails.

But what could he do? Seemed like everbody gathered 'round at Rosie's Restaurant wanted to know—an' they were waitin' to hear it right from the horse's mouth.

"Whaddya say, J.D.?" asked Tumbleweeze. "Are ya goin' to take him on?"

J.D., he sat there a-thinkin'.

"Ya don't need to do it fer my sake," said Rosie, sweet as honey. "He done paid his bill, this time."

"That ain't it!" said one old antelope. "They'll cause all kinds a trouble 'round here, if'n the sheriff don't take the challenge. Y'all know that!"

"They ain't done nothin' but some hootin' an' hollerin' so far," said Rosie. "I'm a-thinkin' they's jest after you this time, J.D.!"

"Don't ya worry yer perty head 'bout me," said J.D.

"Cain't help it," said Rosie, kinda shy-like. ('Course everbody knew they was sweet on each other.)

"J.D., you ain't never let us down before," said Tumbleweeze. (He did tend to say that a good bit, didn't he now?)

"Yeah, J.D.," added Bo. "We's sure you kin do it!"

"Go fer it, Sheriff," said the antelope. "Teach that no-account buffalo an' his gang a lesson like they never learnt before!"

"Sure, you kin take him!" added Tumbleweeze.

"How 'bout that Billy the Kid?" said Bo. "Ya sure did ring his bell!"

Everbody chimed in with that, pattin' J.D. on the back an' all. Rosie, she looked J.D. in the eye an' gave him a wink.

"Don't ferget 'bout Snake-Eye Smith," said Hare-Brain Jack himself.

An' everbody chimed in again.

"Yeah, we ain't had a show like that 'round here in months, J.D." said Bo, kinda wistful.

"An' I love a good rodeo too," added Tumbleweeze. "Anybody else think so?"

"Nothin' better!" said the antelope. (He an' those other deer-folk jest loved a good time.)

Well, there weren't heard a discouragin' word. Seemed like everbody couldn't hardly wait till the big showdown at the ol' Oakey-Dokey next day.

"All right," said J.D. at last. "I'll do it!" An' what a cheer went up from those folks gathered 'round!

Now, ya got to remember that in a place like Dust River Gulch, folks perty much had to make their own excitement. An' J.D., he couldn't deny 'em a good show, now could he?

So just like you'd figger, pert-near the whole town showed up at the corral next day. An' they were jest a-whoopin' it up!

There were banners strung up by the old oak-tree sayin', "*GET 'EM, J.D.!*" an' other such-like stuff.

They even had refreshen-ments! Jack had brought some carrot cake. Rosie, she had some of her famous tomater soup (good as gold, wasn't it?). There were even some leftover bottles of Doc Hardly's all-purpose imported moonbeam-elixir fer sale (dirt cheap, of course).

Gruffle O'Buffalo, he came ridin' inta the corral on the back of those two brahma-bull brothers, one foot on each. An' the crowd started a-booin'.

Bully an' Bully snorted out somethin' fierce right at all them townsfolk, an' everybody quieted down real quick-like.

"Hope yer gonna be good sports!" sneered Gruff. An' them bum steers started up a-snickerin'.

Then J.D. came gallopin' inta the corral. An' the cheerin' commenced. With all that cheerin', J.D. probably thought he could whup 'most anybody—even a cheatin', connivin', lowdown, crim'nal-minded one-ton buffalo with a chip on his mangy shoulder. All of which, an' more, was Gruffle O'Buffalo himself.

Once the cheerin' died down a little, Gruff gave a loud snort an' looked out over the crowd. "Today, we're gonna separate the cowmen from the cowboys!" he said. "This here's the end of the rodeo fer you, Sheriff. We've done had our ridin' competition, but the rodeo ain't over till we done had our ropin'." An' with that, those bum steers started a-hootin' an' a-hollerin' somethin' terrible.

Gruff continued. "Weasel, we'll need yer timin' again. Bully an' Bully'll check on ya—that'll keep things fair an' square. Sheriff, first yer gonna rope me, then I'll rope you, okay?"

"Fair enough," called back J.D.

Tumbleweeze had the contestants take their positions in the gates while he an' the bulls got set fer timin'. 'Course, you

know how ropin' works: the one gittin' roped gits a five-second head start outta the gate. When the timer fires his gun off, then the one doin' the ropin' starts a-chasin him down. Ya has to bring him down with yer rope, then tie up 'least three legs 'fore the timin' stops. At least that's the way it's supposed to work.

Tumbleweeze held his gun straight up in the air an' stared down at his pocketwatch. "Open the gate!" he yelled out. An' out went Gruffle.

Tumbleweeze kept his eye on that pocketwatch. Three—two—one. *Click.*

His gun didn't fire! He tried again—*click. Click, click, click. BANG!* At last!

Nearly twenty seconds went by 'fore J.D. heard the shot to leave his gate!

Meanwhile that one-ton buffalo was a-gallopin way across the big corral like a runaway train.

Tumbleweeze pulled down his gun an' looked it over real puzzled-like. "What's wrong with this thing?" he muttered to himself. An' those bum steers commenced a-snickerin' like maybe they knew.

Well J.D., he had a heap of ground to cover. Gruffle was circlin' 'round at the other side of the corral—way outta ropin' range! So J.D. put on a full gallop. He was a-gainin an' a-gainin'. He pulled out his lasso an' swung it 'round an' 'round over his head an' let it fly. *Thwop*—got that buffalo right around the horns! J.D. pulled that rope tight an' gave it a jerk. But—*snap!*—the rope broke in two!

J.D. could hardly believe it. That rope snapped like it had been cut aforehand! An' wouldn't ya know it, them two bum steers started snickerin' like they knew somethin' 'bout that too. J.D. went chargin' after the rope piece that was dangling from that buffalo's horns. There wasn't more than a few feet left to grab onto. He took a flyin' leap fer the end of that rope an' grabbed it with two hoofs!

"Gotcha, Gruff!" said J.D., grittin' his teeth an'runnin' along behind.

"Ain't down yet!" huffed out Gruffle.

Then Gruff made a sudden stop right in front of J.D. *Ker-BONK*—J.D. smacked right inta a shaggy wall of buffalo hide! Nearly knocked him dizzy, but he held onta that rope. 'Course that might not of been fer the best, 'cause Gruff, he started inta a gallop again. An' J.D., he was draggin' in the dust behind!

That buffalo drug J.D. all over that thar corral. He swung him inta fenceposts along the side. He bumped him over rocks. An' I 'magine J.D. swallered more dust than a turkey in a sandstorm.

But that sheriff didn't let go, no siree! He pulled himself closer and closer on that rope. Perty soon he took a couple of kicks from Gruffle's spurred boots, but that didn't stop him, neither. At last he grabbed hold of Gruff's back legs an' twisted that big ramblin' buffalo down to the ground! *Ker-THUD!* Shook the ground like an earthquake when that buffalo hit the dirt.

J.D. pulled the rest of his rope outta his belt an' tied that buffalo's legs quick as a strikin' rattlesnake. Then he stood up an looked over to Tumbleweeze.

"Two minutes an' twenty-three seconds" announced the weasel.

Well, there was of heap of clappin' fer that performance. Not that the time was so good—it weren't. But J.D. did git that ramblin' ton of buffalo tied up, after all!

After they set a spell, the contestants switched places.

Tumbleweeze reloaded his gun, an' stared down at his pocketwatch again.

"Open the gate!"

Out charged J.D. at full gallop.

Four—three—two—one. *BANG!*

Tumbleweeze pulled down his gun an' looked it over again. "Least it's workin' right now," he muttered to himself.

Meanwhile Gruffle was chasin' after J.D. with his lasso a-swingin'. J.D. dodged right an' he cut to the left.

"Thatta way, J.D.!" yelled out somebody from the crowd.

"Run, J.D., run!"

"Giddyup, J.D.!"

Now Rosie, she noticed somethin' weren't quite right in that thar corral. It seemed like that lasso Gruffle were swingin' 'round wasn't tied right. In fact, the more she looked at that thing, the more she didn't like it. "Why that rope's tied up like a hangman's noose!" she said to herself.

An' so it was!

J.D. switched back an' forth. He turned direction like a twister in a cloud of dust. But finally Gruffle's rope found its mark.

Thwop—aargh! The lasso-noose caught J.D. right around the neck an' stopped him right quick in his tracks!

"I gottcha roped!" said Gruffle. "But ya ain't goin' down—yer goin' up!"

An' with that, the mangy outlaw tossed his rope over a branch in the old oak tree which hung out over the corral. Then the buffalo pulled out the slack. J.D. stood up on his tippy-toes to keep that noose from tightening anymore. All the town folks were struck dumb. They couldn't hardly believe it!

"Now if'n y'all do like I say, maybe I'll let yer sheriff catch his breath a while longer," said Gruffle. "Hardee, har, har! Everbody empty out yer pockets. Boys, go 'round an' collect the goods in yer hats. The big roundup done been turned inta a big holdup—an' of course if'n ya won't cooperate, we'll be stringin' up yer beloved sheriff. Hardee, har."

Well, everbody started pullin' out their money. Ladies took off their jewelry. It mighta been the biggest robbery in the history of Dust River Gulch—'cept fer what happened next.

Now before I git to that, let me tell ya 'bout somethin' I mightta neglected to mention earlier. Now I don't wantta git hung up on this, but I told ya 'bout J.D.'s lookin' fer a deputy, now didn't I? Right, thought so. An' did I tell ya how he didn't find none? Yep. Of course I did. Well, he sure couldda used one now. But ya mighta wondered why he were lookin' fer somebody from outta town. Why not jest hire somebody from right here, in Dust River Gulch?

Well, like I said before, Dust River Gulch always has been a dandy place to live, fer law-abidin' folks, that is. An' there ain't no sheriff west of the Mississippi with a better pedigree than the Gulch's own J.D. Saddlesoap. But he's sorta like a livin' legend nowadays—an' workin' fer a legend, well, that could be a sorta intimidatin' prospect, now couldn't it? Most folks didn't feel like they were deservin' of such an honor. An' of course that left J.D. out on a limb, now, didn't it? That's where we left him too, ain't it? Strung up on that oak tree limb at the Oakey-Dokey Corral.

Well, then it happened!

Whizzzz—there came an arrow a-flyin' through the air. An' *thwip*—it cut right through that rope that J.D. were strung up

by. Quick as a wink, J.D., he untied that noose from 'round his neck an' 'fore Gruff could figger out what was goin' on, he'd been tied up himself!

"Bully! Bully!" called Gruff. "Get after the sheriff!"

An' those two brahma brothers came a-chargin' inta the corral, circlin' 'round on both sides of J.D.

J.D. called out, "Keep that buffalo covered, Deputy, whiles I deal with these two big bullies!" (You were probably wonderin' who that *Deputy* was—you an' most everbody else. But I'll git back to that directly.)

Meanwhiles, Bully an' Bully came a-chargin' at J.D. from both sides. They were snortin' up a storm an' comin' heads down an' horns first! J.D. looked like he was about to become the fillin' inside a brahma-bull sandwich!

He started fer the fence, but them bulls had him in their sights an' they was closin' in—*KER-BLAM*!

I 'magine most everbody closed their eyes fer that crash. But when they opened 'em, there weren't much to see but a big cloud of dust. Well, everbody was a-strainin' to see inta that dust cloud, an' as it slowly cleared away there was a gasp from the crowd.

"Where's J.D.?"

"He's gone!"

"He done vanished!"

Whaddya think they seen? Two groggy-lookin' brahma bulls whose horns were locked together tighter than a jigsaw puzzle! An' there wasn't a trace of J.D. between 'em—er anywheres else!

Well Rosie, she set down that bow an' arrow she were a-pointin' at ol' Gruff, an' she reached fer her hankie.

"Whoa now, Deputy, keep that buffalo in yer sights!"

Yep—It was J.D.! An' where do ya think he was? Sittin' on the limb of that old oak tree!

"J.D.!" said Rosie, about beside herself with all manner of emotions. "How'd you—?"

"Don't know that I kin answer that, Rosie, but here I am!" said J.D. "Kin ya help me git down?"

Then Rosie, she got back to her plucky self again real quick-like, "Not till ya tell what ya mean by callin' me *Deputy*."

"Well, Rosie," said J.D., "I can't think of nobody I'd rather have at my side than you. Will ya be my deputy? An' while yer at it, maybe you'd consider a more personal partnership to boot?"

"J.D. Saddlesoap, are you proposin' to me?" asked Rosie, an' her eyes were sparklin' like a campfire in the moonlight.

"Yes'm," said J.D., out on that limb.

"Somebody git that feller down outta that tree quick!" called out Rosie. "Er I'm goin' up there to set with him!"

"This is downright disgustin'!" called out Gruffle O'Buffalo. "Git me away from these law-enforcin' lovebirds before I gits sick to my stomach all over again!"

Well, the town folks were mighty obligin' to Gruffle's request. They carted him an' his sorry gang of steers right off to the jailhouse. An' those twin brahma bulls with their stuck-together horns? Well, last I heard they were still a-pushin' each other back an' forth across the Texas border.

Meanwhile, back here in Dust River Gulch, things were better than ever. Most anybody'll tell ya—two Saddlesoaps were better than one. An' who knows, maybe there's more to come.

WANTED

GRUFFLE O'BUFFALO

GUILTY OF CRIMES AGAINST THE PEOPLE:

Cattle Rustling, Swindling, Illegal Branding,
Thieving, Lying, Cheating, Loitering,
Humiliating Law Enforcement Agents,
Etc., Etc.

WANTED

BILLY THE KID

GUILTY OF CRIMES AGAINST THE PEOPLE:

Vandalism, Smashing, Tromping, Eating Clothes,
Butting into Innocent Bystanders, General Orneriness,
Humiliating Law Enforcement Agents,
Etc., Etc.

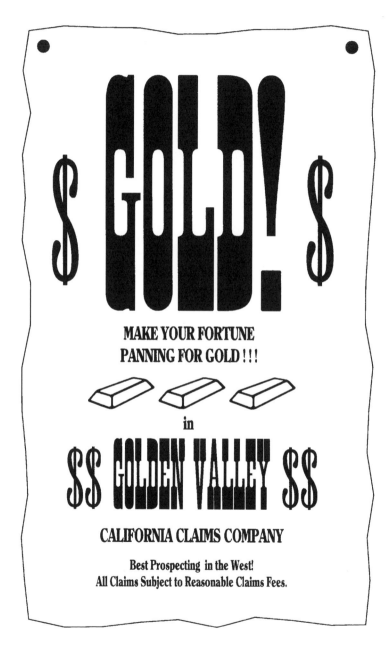